P9-BYN-884

For Jon—
Love, Jessie

SIMON & SCHUSTER BOOKS FOR YOUNG READERS
An imprint of Simon & Schuster Children's Publishing Division
1230 Avenue of the Americas, New York, New York 10020
Copyright © 2018 by Jessie Sima
All rights reserved, including the right of reproduction in whole or in part in any form.
SIMON & SCHUSTER BOOKS FOR YOUNG READERS is a trademark of Simon & Schuster, Inc.
For information about special discounts for bulk purchases, please contact Simon & Schuster
Special Sales at 1-866-506-1949 or business@simonandschuster.com.
The Simon & Schuster Speakers Bureau can bring authors to your live event.
For more information or to book an event, contact the Simon & Schuster Speakers Bureau
at 1-866-248-3049 or visit our website at www.simonspeakers.com.
Book design by Lizzy Bromley • The text for this book was set in Calder.
The illustrations for this book were rendered in Adobe Photoshop.
Manufactured in the United States of America • 1219 PCH
6 8 10 9 7 5
Library of Congress Cataloging-in-Publication Data
Names: Sima, Jessie, author, illustrator.
Title: Love, Z / Jessie Sima.
Description: First edition. | New York : Simon & Schuster Books for Young Readers, [2018] |
Summary: A little robot named Z finds a message in a bottle signed, "Love, Beatrice" and,
unable to learn what love is from other robots, sets out on a quest to find the answer.
Identifiers: LCCN 2017059911 (print) | ISBN 9781481496780 (eBook) | ISBN 9781481496773 (hardcover)
Subjects: | CYAC: Love—Fiction. | Robots—Fiction. | Adventure and adventurers—Fiction.
Classification: LCC PZ7.1.S548 (eBook) | LCC PZ7.1.S548 Lov 2018 (print) | DDC [E]—dc23
LC record available at https://lccn.loc.gov/2017059911

Love, Z

Jessie Sima

Simon & Schuster Books for Young Readers
New York   London   Toronto   Sydney   New Delhi

On a bright, chilly day, Z went out looking for adventure and stumbled upon a piece of half-buried treasure.

Inside was a message, too smudgy to read,
except for two words at the very bottom:

The young robot did not know what "love" meant
or who "Beatrice" was, but they felt important.

So Z tucked the treasure away and headed toward home.

As night fell, all the robots prepared to power down and recharge for the next day.

Z asked for a bedtime story.

And a night-light.

And a good-night kiss.

Tucked snugly in bed,
Z's thoughts drifted back
to the important treasure.

"What is love?"
asked the young robot.

DOES NOT

replied the old, rusty robots.

M

I

Then they said, "Sweet dreams," and turned out the lights.

Alone in the dark, Z could not sleep. The other robots had always been able to answer Z's questions. If they did not know what "love" meant, who would?

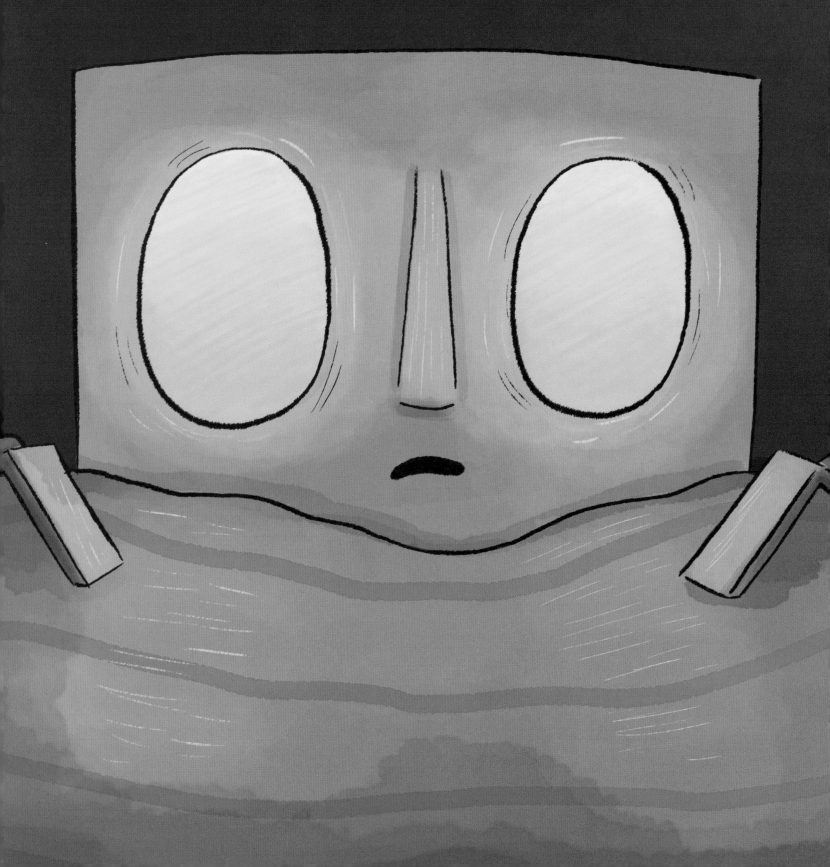

Maybe there was *one* person.

In the morning, Z went out looking for Beatrice.

"Hello, I am looking for Beatrice,"
explained Z. "I want to know what love is,
and she will have the answer."

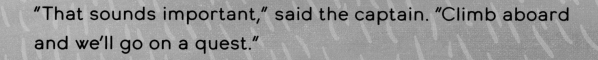

"That sounds important," said the captain. "Climb aboard
and we'll go on a quest."

So they did.

Unsure of how to start a quest, Z asked around.

"Excuse me, are you Beatrice?"

"Are YOU Beatrice?"

"We are on a quest to find out what 'love' is," explained Z. "And Beatrice will have the answer."

"I don't know any Beatrice," said the crow. "But to me . . ."

"Love is sharing your food,
even when it's delicious."

That did not compute. But Z thanked the crow anyway
and changed course toward a place with delicious food.

the Breadboard

The baker did not know Beatrice, either. But she was happy to share what "love" meant to her.

"Love is when someone is patient and takes the time to teach you new things."

That did not compute. But Z thanked the baker anyway and changed course toward a place with teachers.

Absolutely none of them computed. But Z thanked the students anyway, and had no idea what to go in search of.

What if they never found Beatrice?

What if "love" was something a robot just could not compute?

Z was about to suggest that they change course
toward home, when they stumbled upon a good
place to spend the night.

"Hello. We are on a quest—Oh, never mind."

"Hello. I'm Beatrice," said the woman.

"What were you doing out there in the cold?" asked Beatrice.
"Looking for you!" explained Z. "I want to know what 'love' is,
and I thought you would have the answer."
Beatrice paused to think.

She thought.

And thought.

And thought some more.

Z hoped she was right.

"It's getting late," said Beatrice. "Let's get some rest."

The young robot was preparing to power down and recharge for the next day, when . . .

the old, rusty robots
arrived unannounced!

"Z! You were gone. We were worried."

"But we found you."

"We brought your favorite bedtime story."

"And your night-light."

"And a good-night kiss."

Tucked snugly in bed, Z felt warm.
And cozy. And safe.

It was a feeling the
young robot had felt
many times before. . . .

But now it had a name.